GALAXY ZACK

Snow Place Like Home

By Ray O'Ryan

Illustrated by Jason Kraft

LITTLE SIMON

New York   London   Toronto   Sydney   New Delhi

LITTLE SIMON
An imprint of Simon & Schuster Children's Publishing Division
1230 Avenue of the Americas, New York, New York 10020
First Little Simon hardcover edition October 2018
Copyright © 2018 by Simon & Schuster, Inc.
Also available in a Little Simon paperback edition.
All rights reserved, including the right of reproduction in whole or in part in any form.
LITTLE SIMON is a registered trademark of Simon & Schuster, Inc., and associated
colophon is a trademark of Simon & Schuster, Inc. For information about special discounts
for bulk purchases, please contact Simon & Schuster Special Sales at 1-866-506-1949 or
business@simonandschuster.com. The Simon & Schuster Speakers Bureau can bring authors to
your live event. For more information or to book an event contact the Simon & Schuster Speakers
Bureau at 1-866-248-3049 or visit our website at www.simonspeakers.com.
Designed by Nick Sciacca
Manufactured in the United States of America 0918 FFG
1 2 3 4 5 6 7 8 9 10
This book has been cataloged with the Library of Congress.
ISBN 978-1-5344-2905-5 (pbk)
ISBN 978-1-5344-2906-2 (hc)
ISBN 978-1-5344-2907-9 (eBook)

CONTENTS

Chapter 1

Frozanthia, Here We Come!

Zack Nelson and Drake Taylor were surrounded by a towering mountain of clothes. The Nelson's were going on a family winter vacation to Frozanthia, a snowy ice planet in the Frostus Galaxy.

"I'm so glad you're coming with us, Drake," said Zack.

The boys had been best friends
since Zack moved to Nebulon.

"Me too, I am so excited!" Drake
agreed. "Frozanthia has grape out-
door adventures!"

"You're not kidding!" said Zack. "I mean, look at this holo-brochure!"

He held up his hyperphone and a 3-D hologram of a gleaming, icy landscape filled the room.

A snow-bot with
a set of hydro-jets
appeared.

"Hi, Zack and Drake!
Welcome to your virtual
tour! There's *snow* place
like the Polar Palace
Resort in the entire
galaxy!" it said.

"You will enjoy solar-snowboarding on Frost Mountain, hydro-freeze fishing on Invisible Lake, snow fort building, a winter arcade, and an out-of-this-world five-star restaurant! Safe travels, and remember to bundle up!"

"You bet!" the boys exclaimed. Then the snow-bot waved good-bye and the hologram shut off.

"The resort looks amazing! I can't wait to go solar-snowboarding!" Zack cried as Mrs. Nelson walked in.

"Well, if you want go snow-boarding for real, you'd better get busy!" she said.

"Don't worry, Mom. We have got this all under control," Zack told her.

His mom smiled as she closed the door. The boys stared up at the clothes pile. It almost touched the ceiling.

"Ira!" Zack called. "Help before there's an underwear avalanche!"

"Not to worry, Master Just Zack," said Ira, the Nelsons' Indoor Robotic Assistant.

Mechanical arms dropped from the ceiling and started folding clothes in a blur. Within seconds, everything fit into two shrink-sacs. Ira pressed a button on each piece of luggage. The large bags shook, then shrunk down to the size of a wallet.

"Thanks, Ira!" Zack said with a sigh of relief.

Drake excitedly waved good-bye to Ira. "Frozanthia, here we come!"

Chapter 2

Polar Palace Resort

Zack pressed his face against the window of their space cruiser. Stars shined brightly against the black sky. He loved flying, no matter where he went.

Soon, a sparkling white landscape appeared. Zack's sisters gazed out

the window. They had finally reached
Frozanthia.

"The planet . . ."

". . . looks like a giant . . ."

". . . snowball!" shouted the twins.

The cruiser landed at the spaceport
and the family hopped into an ice pod
to go to the resort. Ice pods were similar

to cruisers on Nebulon, but they had skates on the bottom to travel across the frozen roads. Once everyone was buckled in, their driver released the brakes and zoomed into the falling snow.

Zack looked out the window and admired the majestic snowcapped mountains in the distance. As the snow cleared, Zack noticed an ice-covered hotel with giant wood doors at the front gate. A sign nailed into the ice read POLAR PALACE RESORT.

"Wow, this place is built entirely with ice blocks!" Zack exclaimed.

A snow-bot stood at the entrance. When the ice pod stopped, the snow-bot opened the door. "Welcome to Polar Palace Resort, Nelson family and Mr. Drake Taylor! Please follow me."

The snow-bot pressed a button on its head and the gigantic wood doors slid open. A ski lift was waiting on the other side. It had wide, comfy seats, large windows, and two ice wings.

"This lift will take you directly to your room. I do hope you enjoy your stay!"

The family climbed in and lifted into the air. The cold felt good on Zack's face. From above the trees, he could see that each floor of the resort was different. One floor was lined with cozy log cabins, while another had sparkling crystal igloo rooms. When they reached the top floor, Zack couldn't believe his eyes. They were staying in an awesome snowcapped tree house!

He burst through the door and saw a holo-display that showed three levels of fun.

"Look! There's something here for all of us!" Mrs. Nelson said excitedly. "Even a spa for me!"

The twins raced up to the canopy ice beds that hovered on the second floor. Their bedroom had a wall-to-wall vidscreen and a swinging bench.

The boys' room was on the third floor, and it had two ice pod beds! Next to each pod, a smooth ramp dipped down to the first floor.

"This is so grape!" Drake cried.

"Yippee wah-wah! It's the indoor ski jump!" Zack yelled.

The two friends zoomed off the ramp and landed safely on a big, comfy couch.

Zack called to his mom. "Can we *please* play a few games at the winter arcade?" he begged.

"Okay, but take these. Remember, we have dinner reservations in an hour," his mom said. She handed them each a wristband. The devices lit up as soon as they put them on.

"Hello, I am Pat, your Portable Assisting Technology unit," a voice said. "If you need anything during your stay, just say my name."

"Grape!" said Drake and Zack at the same time.

"Nice to meet you, Pat! How do we get to the winter arcade?" Zack asked.

"I'd be happy to escort you," Pat replied. "A ski lift is waiting outside."

Chapter 3
Winter Arcade

The Winter Arcade was an enormous sparkling cave. Tall icicles hung from the ceiling and colorful lights reflected around the room.

A boy with soft blue fur and big round eyes greeted Zack and Drake at the front desk.

"Hi! My name is Jaxon," he said.

"I'm Zack, and this is Drake," he said, pointing to his best friend. "We're here to play some games!"

"Great! My sister and I can show you around!" replied Jaxon as a tiny flying bot scanned their wrists.

"Now you can play any game you want!" said the girl next to him. "My name is Ava."

The arcade was filled with several rows of game pods. The siblings led the boys to one called Frost Mountain Solar Blast.

When the game turned on, they were transported to Frost Mountain, with full snow gear and helmets. Drake felt the snow crunch under his feet and the wind whip against his face. "This is amazing!" he said. "It feels like I am really standing in snow!"

"I'm sure we'll get the hang of it," Zack said confidently.

Ava pointed out that there were two difficulty settings: easy or advanced. The boys decided to try the easy course first, and obstacles instantly appeared on the mountain.

"That's because this video game of Frost Mountain is supposed to feel real!" explained Jaxon.

"All the games at this arcade were built to help kids practice," Ava added. "Solar-snowboarding is harder than it looks."

Zack took a deep breath as the kids lined up.

"On your mark... Get set... Go!" Jaxon yelled.

Zack leaned forward and sped down as fast as he could. He was amazed at how real everything felt.

His board glided smoothly on the snow. Then, at a sharp curve, he turned to the right, easily jumped over a log, and landed back down with a soft *whoosh!* He moved swiftly past every obstacle and arrived at the bottom in first place! Drake finished closely behind him.

"Wow, is it really your first time?" Jaxon asked when he arrived a few seconds later.

"Yeah, it was!" Zack replied. "Let's go again!"

The game reset and they were instantly back at the top of the mountain. After several runs, the kids moved on to solar ski jumping and extreme solar sledding. Just like the first game, Zack and Drake adjusted quickly and beat each round with ease. Zack was having so much fun that he didn't notice his wristband was flashing.

"Hello, Zack," said Pat. "It's time to meet your family for dinner."

"Thanks, Pat," replied Zack. "We're on our way."

The kids left the game and made plans to meet the next day. If the arcade was built to help kids practice, then Zack was sure tomorrow would be a breeze!

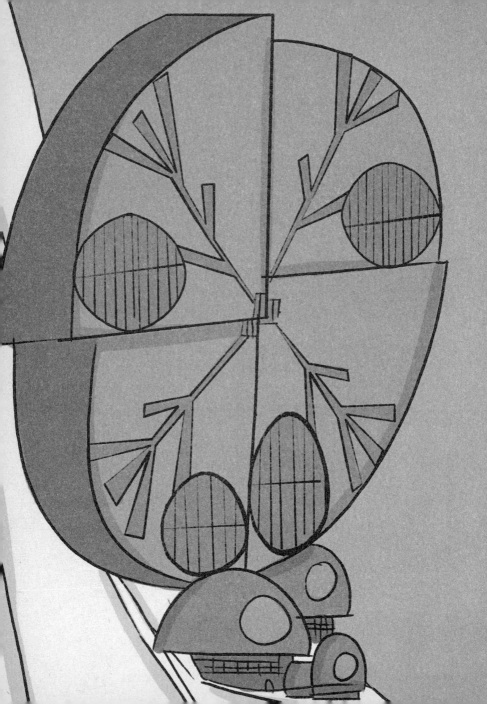

Chapter 4
Snowflake Café

A hostess greeted the family at the entrance to the restaurant. "Welcome to Snowflake Café. Is this your first time with us?"

"It sure is," replied Mr. Nelson.

"Wow, this place looks like a giant snowflake Ferris wheel!" said Zack.

Many long crystal spokes connected each dining room to the center of the moving wheel. That was where the kitchen was.

"Great! Your dining room is here now," said the hostess as she pointed to an egg-shaped glass pod. The doors slid open, and they took their seats at a table for six. Colorful snowflakes danced along the glass walls.

"It's like being inside . . ."

". . . a snow globe!" exclaimed the twins.

When the doors shut, another snow-bot with long limbs appeared. He had on a clear, sparkling suit of ice that showed all the wires connected in his body.

"Select any picture to pull up a sensory 4-D hologram of a dish," he announced.

"You will be able to see, smell, and sample everything on the menu."

Once everyone tried a few meals, the snow-bot took their orders.

"I would like the snowball mashed potatoes, please," said Drake.

"And I'll have the let it snow-cakes!" said Zack.

"Toasted marshmallow mac 'n' cheese . . ."

". . . and frosted fries for us, please!" said the twins.

Zack's mouth started to water. He couldn't wait to try everything! Even the chilled chicken frosty and ice fish soufflé his parents ordered sounded delicious.

41

"Excellent choices!" said the snow-bot as a panel on the ceiling opened. White snowflakes and sprinkles drifted softly down onto Zack's empty plate, forming two fluffy cakes. Then, right after, the snow-bot launched two giant snowballs from his hands.

"Duck!" Zack yelled as the balls zoomed right over Drake's head. The boys watched excitedly as the bot hit the snowballs back and forth across the room before they landed neatly on Drake's plate.

"That was so grape, but way too close!" Drake said with a laugh.

Then three new snow-bots appeared in the room. They stood on one another's shoulders and began doing acrobatic flips and tricks while preparing the rest of the family's food.

"This pod will now detach from the kitchen," said one of the bots. "Enjoy the beautiful view during your meal."

Their pod left its base and flew into the frosty mountains. Everyone eagerly dug in to their food.

"This might be my new favorite restaurant!" exclaimed Zack.

"Me too! No wonder this place is known all over the galaxy," Drake agreed.

Zack quickly cleaned his entire plate and got ready for dessert. As he dug in to a giant snowberry flurrado, he looked out the window and admired the gorgeous view. Frozanthia was really turning out to be the best place ever!

Chapter 5

Frost Mountain

Early the next morning, Zack and Drake met Jaxon and Ava at the base of Frost Mountain.

"Are you ready?" asked Jaxon.

"You bet!" said Zack confidently.

A snow-bot at the rental center gave out solar boots and helmets.

"Wow, this stuff sure is heavy!" Drake said.

"That's because the gravity down here is much stronger than the gravity in the mountains," Ava explained. "You will need the extra weight to ski down the slopes."

Jaxon nodded. "Now remember, there are two difficulty settings. When you select one, your helmet will show you the path."

"Awesome, let's go straight to the advanced slope!" exclaimed Zack.

The boys put on their boots and suddenly their wristbands began to beep. A soft glow surrounded them like another layer of clothing.

"What is this?" asked Drake as he looked at his hands.

"That is your force field," said Ava.

"It protects you in case you fall."

"We're not going to fall," said Zack with a wink. "Right, Drake?"

The blue Nebulon smiled nervously. "Right. Now, how do we get to the top of the mountain?"

"Simple!" said Jaxon. "Just say 'Lift me up, Pat!'"

Jaxon disappeared as soon as he said the words. Zack and Drake stared at each other in disbelief. Then they tried it, and a glittering light beamed around them.

When the light
was gone, Zack and
Drake were no longer
in the rental center. They
stood in the snow on top of
the highest mountain.

Drake gulped as he stared
down the steep winding trail. "Wow,
the advanced slope is a lot higher than
I expected."

Ava appeared next to him. "We can switch to the easy slopes if you want."

"Don't worry, Drake. We got this!" Zack said with a smile. His friend's excitement helped Drake loosen up.

"All right, be careful!" said Jaxon. "We'll see you at the bottom!"

Then Jaxon and Ava leaned forward and a laser snowboard erupted from their solar boots. They effortlessly sped down the trail. As Zack watched them zoom away, he took a deep breath and bent forward too. At first he thought he was going to fall, then his own laser snowboard sparked to life.

Zack sailed down the mountain. He began to relax as he took in his surroundings.

The path was lined with tall, beautiful snow-covered trees, just like in the arcade game.

He looked over his shoulder and saw Drake next to him. He gave his friend a quick nod and they both leaned harder against the wind.

Suddenly warning lights flashed across Zack's visor. A steep jump was ahead. Zack tried to swerve toward the snow ramp, but it felt like his board was controlling him! Before he knew it, Zack hit the jump and went flying into the air.

Drake flew out of control right behind him. Their laser snowboards retracted back into their boots before they landed in the soft snow.

"Owww!" Drake cried out in pain. "My ankle!"

Zack rushed over to his friend just
as a safety alarm sounded. It was
Drake's wristband!

"Don't worry. I'm scanning your
ankle," said Pat. A light rippled from
Drake's bracelet. "It looks like a minor
sprain. A rescue-bot will be here to
help in three, two, one."

A bot that looked like a dog came blasting out of the snowy woods. Using its mechanical teeth, the rescue-bot carefully wrapped bandages around Drake's ankle.

Then a sled unfolded and Zack helped his friend onto it. "So, that was nothing like yesterday, huh?"

"Yeah, it is *snow* wonder we wiped out," Drake replied with a smile.

Zack let out a halfhearted laugh as the recue-bot moved forward, escorting them both safely down the mountain. This vacation was definitely not starting on the right foot.

Chapter 6
Invisible Lake

With Drake's hurt ankle, solar-snowboarding was out of the question. So early the next morning, the kids gathered at Invisible Lake to go hydro-freeze fishing. Lots of other kids were already there, standing by holes on the frozen lake.

Zack, Drake, Jaxon, Ava, and the twins looked into the lake. There were robo-fish swimming underneath the ice.

"This is so grape!" said Zack. "But we won't fall in, right?"

"Of course not!" Jaxon cheered. "Invisible Lake is always frozen solid. How is your ankle, Drake?"

"It is feeling better already,"

said Drake. "Plus, this crystal boot helps."

"Perfect!" said Ava. "So let me tell you about hydro-freeze fishing. You each have an aqua-line built in to your Pat. Cast it into one of these holes like this."

Ava flicked her wrist like she was throwing a yo-yo. A sparkling crystal line sputtered out from her bracelet and landed in the water with a plop.

"Your aqua-line attracts robo-fish," explained Jaxon. "When you feel a tug, press the red button to catch it. Each person can catch only one fish."

Zack frowned. "Only one fish? Why? I want to catch a million!"

Jaxon laughed. "It's a surprise, Zack! I'll explain more when you have your robo-fish."

The kids split up and began fishing. Within seconds, Cathy and Charlotte

felt a hard tug on their lines. They pressed their buttons, and two nets with shiny robo-fish rose the top of the water.

"Hey! These robo-fish have mirrored scales . . ."

". . . and they dance!" exclaimed the twins. "Wow, you caught disco fish!" Ava said.

The twins scooped up their nets and admired their first catch.

Soon after, Jaxon and Ava caught robo-fish with intricate scale designs.

"Hey! We caught maze mystery fish!" Ava gave her brother a high five.

Meanwhile, Zack and Drake's crystal aqua-lines had not moved at all. The boys sat quietly. Then, after a while, Drake's line tugged.

"Yippee wah-wah! I got one!" he cried.

Drake pulled his crystal net out of the water and opened it. It was a giant robo-fish with wheels!

"That's a race-car fish!" said Jaxon. Drake grinned. He packed his robo-fish away and sat next to his friend.

Zack sat back and hung his head. Everyone else around him was having much better luck.

Kids cheered loudly every time they caught a fish. But Zack's aqua-line remained still as time dragged on.

"Gosh, whoever said fishing was fun?" asked Zack exhaustedly.

"Hmm, maybe the fish fell asleep?" Drake replied. "WAKE UP, FISH!"

Zack was ready to give up when he saw a large ripple form in the water. "I got something!"

He quickly pressed his button and pulled up the crystal net. Zack yanked with all his might as a clump of sticky, white seaweed rose out of Invisible Lake! It was squishy and gross.

"What kind of fish is this?" he asked.

Ava and Jaxon only shrugged. Zack went to throw the gunk back into the water, but Jaxon stopped him. "Wait! You never know what might come in handy when building an ice fort."

Zack raised his eyebrow and gave his new friends a curious look. "Did you say 'ice fort'?"

Chapter 7

Ice Fort Disaster

Ava and Jaxon led the others to the Frozanthia Ice Flats. It was a wide-open field surrounded by tall, towering trees and beautiful hills. A group of floating drone-bots spelled out "Ice Fort Party" in the sky.

"Here's the surprise," said Jaxon.

"Frozanthia is having an ice fort contest!"

"That is grape, but what does an ice fort have to do with robo-fish?" asked Drake.

"The type of robo-fish you catch should match the type of ice fort you build," explained Ava. "Jaxon and I caught maze fish, so we will build an ice maze."

"Yay! Our ice fort will have . . ."

". . . a rockin' dance floor!" the twins cried.

The kids scattered to start building, but Zack stayed put. "What kind of ice fort can I build with seaweed?" he asked.

Drake smiled and put his arm around his friend. "A great one, if you work with me!"

Zack smiled. Even with a hurt foot, Drake was always there to help. They took out his robo-fish and it instantly split into a snow-bot crew! The snow-bots began to smooth the ground for a racetrack so they could build an ice wall around it.

Zack pulled out the seaweed and tossed it on the ground. "Looks like I won't need this anymore."

As the bots shaped the snow, Zack pointed to where each block should be placed. The snow-bots worked quickly. Zack watched as they stacked blocks until they had made a wall. The ice fort was starting to take shape.

Then an alarm blared. "SYSTEM ERROR! SYSTEM ERROR!"

A snow-bot was stuck in Zack's seaweed! He tried to help free it, but with every push, the bot dug deeper into the sticky gunk. Soon, another alarm echoed throughout the fort.

"Oh no! Another snow-bot is stuck!"
Zack cried.

Drake quickly grabbed one of the
bot's arms. "We can pull them out."

Zack nodded as the boys pulled as
hard as they could. Something came
loose as they all tumbled backward.

83

One of the robot's arms flew over their heads and crashed through their ice wall.

"Oh no! We have lost two snow-bots." Drake frantically tried to repair the damage.

Zack watched his friend try to fix things as he snuck away quietly. "This is all my fault. First I hurt Drake's leg, and then I break his fort. He'll be much better off without unlucky me on his team."

Chapter 8

May the Best Fort Win!

Zack walked over to Jaxon and Ava's maze fort. The ice path went in every direction. It was the perfect place to get lost, so Zack stepped inside.

A long narrow passageway led to an ice bench. Zack sat down, and it immediately collapsed!

"Aw man," Zack muttered.

His wristband lit up. It was Pat. "Is everything okay, Zack?"

"Yes, I'm fine," said Zack. "It's just that none of these winter games are playing out like I thought they would."

"Well then, why not change your game plan?" Pat suggested.

Zack shook his head. "Thanks, but trust me. I'll just make things worse."

Then there was a shuffling sound as Ava came around the corner. "Hey, Zack. What are you doing here?"

"I needed to find some place out of the way," he said. "I almost ruined our entire fort!"

"Well, that makes two of us!" Ava sat down next to him and pointed to a map of their fort. "We're rebuilding these pathways for the third time!"

"Really?" Zack was surprised. "But your fort looks amazing!"

"Thanks! Let me tell you, building this maze has been so a-maze-ingly difficult!" she replied. "In fact, even I was lost in here until I heard your voice!"

"What? No way!" Zack cried.

"Yeah, I'm lucky I stumbled into you," Ava admitted. "You make a great teammate!"

"Well, you too!" Zack said as they got up from the floor. A huge grin spread across his face. "Guess I'm not so unlucky after all!"

"I'd say you're good luck!" Ava gave him a pat on the back. "May the best fort win!"

Zack nodded, and then he rushed out the door to get back to work.

Chapter 9
And the Winner Is . . .

Back at Drake's fort, total chaos had broken out. Snowballs were flying in all directions and gigantic holes and cracks covered the walls. The snow-bots were having a massive battle!

Zack found Drake sitting behind one of the ice walls. He rushed over and

crouched next to him. Zack peeked through a hole in the wall, then quickly ducked as a snowball zoomed by his head.

"Wow, that was a close one!" Zack exclaimed. "What happened?"

"Oh, there you are! The bots have gone haywire! What do we do, Zack?" Drake asked worriedly.

Zack looked around and spotted a glob of gross, gunky seaweed. Right then, the perfect idea hit him like a snowball.

"Hey, Pat! Can you power down our snow-bots?" Zack called out.

"Sure thing!" Pat replied. All the bots immediately stopped in their tracks.

"Smart thinking," said Drake. "But who will fix the fort now?"

"We will with this." Zack leaned over and grabbed the seaweed. "We can patch the holes in the fort! That is, if you still want me on your team."

"Yippee wah-wah, of course!" Drake cried.

Zack and Drake were admiring their fort when the others stopped by to check on them.

"Wow, this ice fort contest is *snow*

joke," Zack said. "I wish there was a way we could all win."

"That would be, as you say, grape!" agreed Jaxon.

"Hmm. What if we do not have to compete against one another?" asked Drake as he studied all three forts.

"We could connect our forts to make one giant fort."

"Then our fort would become the ultimate . . ."

". . . winter adventure!" cried the twins.

Everyone got to work. Ava and
Jaxon's snow-bots built a slide to
connect the boys' fort to theirs. Then
the twins built a walkway bridge to link
their fort too.

They all finished just as the judging
was about to start.

"Hey, we did it! Now let's make sure
it works!" said Ava. The kids rushed
into Drake and Zack's racing fort first.

Zack grabbed
an ice sled and leaned
forward. After three quick laps
around the track, he zoomed onto
the connecting slide and entered the
maze. All his friends came through one
by one right after him.

Once in Jaxon and Ava's fort, they
took the lead. After several dead ends,
they found the twin's walkway that led

to a sparkling dance floor. Colorful
disco lights swept across the room,
and music blasted from ice speakers.
All the kids bounced around happily,
even Drake!

"Yippee wah-wah!" Zack cried out.

"We are *so* going to win!"

Chapter 10
Snow Place Like Home

When the judges arrived, they were very surprised by the size of the kids' fort. As they stepped inside, Zack waited nervously.

When the judges came out, their hair was wind-whipped from the racetrack, maze-adventure, and wild dance party.

"That was very impressive," said the head judge. "We have never seen teams work together in this way. Thank you."

The judges left and Zack and his friends hugged one another.

"Even if we don't win, I had a great time," said Zack. "Thanks for showing us around, Jaxon and Ava. You are full of surprises."

Drake nodded. "Yes, and thank you for helping me out of your maze. I was so lost in there."

Ava and Jaxon looked at each other and smiled. "Um, we have one more surprise left."

Jaxon whispered into his wristband, "Pat, please send out a message to all the other builders on the Ice Flats: Who would like to join all the forts together?"

Instantly a burst of holo-emoticons beamed into the air. Kragulon smiley faces, Olfo three-thumbs-up, and Slimesly sparkle fireworks hovered over the field. The crowd roared with excitement.

"Looks like a yes?" asked Drake.

"Correct,"
answered his own
Pat. "All the players
would like to join you in
creating the biggest ice fort
in Frozanthia history."

"Well then, we better get started!"
cheered Zack.

Kids from all over
the galaxy connected
the forts. There was
a long, winding slide
that moved in and out
of each ice wall. Even
the snow-bots looked
like they were
enjoying the
forts!

But by far, everyone's favorite space
was the twins' dance floor fort. Even
Zack's parents boogied to the music.
It was epic.

Later that night, the friends met by the winter bonfire. A transparent dome covered the blue flames, and a soft warmth spread around all of them.

"I can't believe we're heading back tomorrow," said Zack. "I had such a great time here, thanks to you guys."

"We did too!" Jaxon agreed.

Then Ava pulled out a marker. "There's just one thing left to do. We need to sign Drake's crystal boot!"

"Oh, that would be awesome!" agreed Drake.

Ava wrote her name in bold letters while Jaxon drew a race-car robo-fish. Even the twins signed Drake's boot, drawing a disco-dancing snowflake.

When it was Zack's turn, he wrote a poem:

> *Snowflakes are cold,*
> *Bonfire's blue,*
> *Frozanthia's great*
> *Because I'm here with you.*

"Thanks, Zack!" said Drake. "I hope
we come back soon. I will use the easy
track next time."

Everyone laughed.

Then Zack said, "Jaxon and Ava, you should visit Nebulon sometime. I'd love to show you around our planet. We can play grape games, ride Nebulon bikes, and eat boingoberry jam!"

As Zack and Drake named fun things to do on Nebulon, the friends sat together under the frozen night sky with shooting stars that looked like falling snow.